WITHDRAWN

True Stories
Of Animal Heroes

Onyx

True Stories
of Animal Heroes

Onyx

Vita Murrow   Anneli Bray

Frances Lincoln
Children's Books

For seventy long years, the mountains of Yellowstone were empty of wolves. The plants and animals were out of balance without them. Until one day, they made a triumphant return. Every ridge was soon protected by its own pack.

Yet, it wasn't always safe to be a new wolf in an old land. Some humans didn't like their presence. In one wolf family, hunters stole the father away in the night. Leaving the mother and her pups alone.

Luckily, the pups were gutsy just like Mum.
All except for one...Onyx.

When the pups raced at food, Onyx hung back.

When the pups wrestled, Onyx stood aside.

The pups were strong and bold, but Onyx was small and shy.
This made life harder for him.

But it also meant that, when the time came
for Onyx to go out into the world, he took
with him a special way of thinking.

One day Onyx met a family just like his own.
A lone mother wolf, with pups. It was the first
time he had seen wolves smaller than him!

Instead of fighting, Onyx played with the pups. They had never seen another grown-up wolf before. They didn't know that he was unique from other alpha wolves.

The pups called Onyx 'Father'. And he was glad to be one.
Especially to the smallest pup, Bravo.
Bravo was strong in body and personality.

Bravo pushed back and charged ahead.

Bravo struggled to listen.

Sometimes Bravo would bite, snarl and sulk.

Onyx coached Bravo to see the world in new ways.

Onyx reminded Bravo to be generous,
even if he didn't feel like sharing.

To be understanding even when things weren't fair.

And Onyx taught Bravo to see that
even when he felt alone, he wasn't.

When Bravo left for the wide world,
he found a partner and a pack of his own.

As happens in every great wolf's life, the time came for Bravo to show himself to be a leader. He was responsible for his own territory and he was expected to attack any wolf who crossed his ridge.

One day, an old wolf approached.
Bravo readied for an attack...

But as the wolf came closer, Bravo saw it was his father, Onyx. He didn't know what to do.

He planned to snarl and growl, attack and defend.
But with the eyes of Onyx upon him, Bravo
remembered his father's special way of thinking.

Bravo bowed his head low. His long nose brushed the ground. It was a gesture of honour that told everyone there was a new way to rule: not through force, but with respect. Onyx passed freely.

In time, this new way of thinking passed on to all of the wolves in the pack. And Bravo's ridge was a place for any wolf who dared to be different.

Did you know this book is based on the real-life story of wolves in the northern mountains of Yellowstone Park?

Yellowstone is a national park in the western United States. In 1926, human use of the land caused the wolves to disappear.

Fortunately, in 1995 human helpers brought 41 wolves from Canada to start a new life in the park. The wolves helped increase the movement and population of many animals, willow trees and other plants. The sounds of howling returned once more.

One of the wolves from this project was Wolf 8, whom we named 'Onyx' for this book. His story was observed by wolf watchers and wildlife biologists, who tracked and cheered on the wolves.

They followed Wolf 8 as he grew up and found a family. Then, too, the youngest of his pups, Wolf 21 or 'Bravo' as we called him in our story, grew up to be a leader who broke the mould. Or, 'began a new legacy'.

You can help ensure wolves stay a part of nature's balance by learning about and supporting wolf projects and the endangered species laws that protect animals and nature.

www.yellowstone.org/wolf-project/

Brimming with creative inspiration, how-to projects, and useful information to enrich your everyday life, Quarto Knows is a favourite destination for those pursuing their interests and passions. Visit our site and dig deeper with our books into your area of interest: Quarto Creates, Quarto Cooks, Quarto Homes, Quarto Lives, Quarto Drives, Quarto Explores, Quarto Gifts, or Quarto Kids.

Text © 2021 Vita Murrow. Illustrations © 2021 Anneli Bray.
First published in 2021 by Frances Lincoln Children's Books,
an imprint of The Quarto Group.
The Old Brewery, 6 Blundell Street, London N7 9BH, United Kingdom.
T (0)20 7700 6700 F (0)20 7700 8066 www.QuartoKnows.com
A catalogue record for this book is available from the British Library.
ISBN 978-0-7112-6143-3
Set in Quicksand and Gathenbury Typeface
Published by Katie Cotton
Designed by Karissa Santos
Edited by Katy Flint
Production by Dawn Cameron

Manufactured in China CC122020
9 8 7 6 5 4 3 2 1

Also in the **True Stories of Animal Heroes** series:

Fluffles

978-0-7112-6157-0

The BRAVE koala who held strong through a bushfire

Read about Fluffles, the koala, who held on through the bushfires in South Australia with bravery. While she healed, she found other koalas to snuggle up with. Their cuddles for one another helped make the whole outback feel better.

This huggable story has a fact section at the back, so you can learn more about koalas and how you can help them.